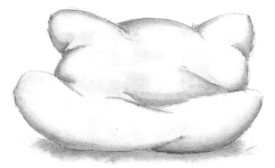

For the real Lucky

First published 1995 by Walker Books Ltd
87 Vauxhall Walk, London SE11 5HJ

This edition published 2009

2 4 6 8 10 9 7 5 3 1

© 1995 Nigel McMullen

The right of Nigel McMullen to be identified as author/illustrator of this work
has been asserted by him in accordance with the Copyright, Designs and Patents Act 1988

This book has been typeset in Garamond Educational

Printed in China

British Library Cataloguing in Publication Data:
a catalogue record for this book is available from the British Library.

ISBN 978-0-7445-3537-2

www.walker.co.uk

Lucky the Puppy

Nigel McMullen

WALKER BOOKS

AND SUBSIDIARIES

LONDON • BOSTON • SYDNEY • AUCKLAND

Lucky the puppy
loves to play.

She runs and jumps
and splashes all day.

Lucky the puppy
loves sticks to chase,

balls to bounce,
friends to race,

paper to tear,
slippers to chew,

comfy chairs –
pillows too!

Lucky the puppy
loves biscuits for tea,

but best of all,
Lucky loves me!

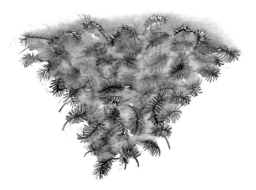